THE INTERNET LIBRARY

Communicating on the Internet

Art Wolinsky

Enslow Publishers, Inc.

40 Industrial Road	PO Box 38
Box 398	Aldershot
Berkeley Heights, NJ 07922	Hants GU12 6BP
USA	UK

http://www.enslow.com

Books in THE INTERNET LIBRARY series

Communicating
on the Internet
Paperback 0-7660-1743-5
Library Ed. 0-7660-1260-3

The History of the Internet
and the World Wide Web
Paperback 0-7660-1746-X
Library Ed. 0-7660-1261-1

Creating and Publishing
Web Pages
on the Internet
Paperback 0-7660-1744-3
Library Ed. 0-7660-1262-X

Locating and Evaluating
Information
on the Internet
Paperback 0-7660-1745-1
Library Ed. 0-7660-1259-X

Library of Congress Cataloging-in-Publication Data

Wolinsky, Art.
    Communicating on the Internet / Art Wolinsky.
       p. cm. — (The Internet library)
    Includes bibliographical references.
    Summary: Explains the different means of communication available
on the Internet, including e-mail, search engines, and chat rooms.
    ISBN 0-7660-1743-5 (pbk)
    ISBN 0-7660-1260-3 (library ed.)
    1. Internet (Computer network) Juvenile literature. [1. Internet
(Computer network)] I. Title II. Series
TK5105.875.I57W63   1999
004.67′8—dc21   99-12746
                                         CIP

Printed in the United States of America

10 9 8 7 6 5 4 3

To Our Readers:
All Internet addresses in this book were active and appropriate when we
went to press. Any comments or suggestions can be sent by e-mail to
Comments@enslow.com or to the address on the back cover.

Trademarks:
Most computer and software brand names have trademarks or registered
trademarks. The individual trademarks have not been listed here.

Cover Photo: Index Stock Photography, Inc./Lisa Podgur Cuscuna

Contents

Introduction

This is my friend Web. He will be appearing throughout the pages of this book to guide you through the information presented here and to take you to a variety of Internet sites and activities. Web is also a reminder that there is always more to learn about the Internet.

There are books to teach you how to use Netscape e-mail. There are books to teach you how to use Microsoft Exchange e-mail, and there are books to teach you how to use Eudora mail. This is not one of those books. This is not a book on how to use software.

In order to teach you how to use e-mail software, you would need an Internet connection, but you do not need an Internet connection to use this book. The focus is on how to communicate effectively and how to use the power of online communication as a tool in your life. You will learn how online communication is different from other forms of communication, and you will learn fine points of Internet communication citizenship. Online communication can help you with your schoolwork and in your personal life. It can help you prepare for your future or prepare for a party. It can put you in touch with friends, professionals, and people all over the world, but only if you know how to ensure that people will want to read what you send.

Knowing how to use e-mail software without knowing what it can do for you, or how to use it to communicate effectively, is like knowing how to drive a car but not knowing how to get to where you want to go. Knowing how to click on a send button will do you no good unless you know how and where to contact people. In short, knowing how to use e-mail software will do no good unless you know how to communicate in ways that encourage others to write back.

We can never know everything, and I certainly cannot put everything in this book. I will, however, provide you with Internet URLs where you can find additional information about the topics I cover. URL stands for uniform resource locator. It is an Internet address you type into your Web browser. In this case the URLs will point you to some online e-mail tutorials that will show you the ins and outs of different e-mail software.

Starting All Over:
E-mail is a great way to communicate with someone, but first we need to learn how to communicate effectively.

Internet Addresses   Communication Facts   How Can I Be Safe?

The first URL (Internet address) on the following list leads to a tutorial about Dominant Mail, a simple mail program that has many of the features found in today's popular software.

<http://www.magpie.org/life/student/immersion/mail/
   tutorial1.html>

Eudora has long been the leader in Internet e-mail.

Eudora Lite for Windows:
<http://www.emailman.com/eudora/win/info.html>

Eudora Lite for Mac:
<http://www.emailman.com/eudora/mac/info.html>

Today's Web browsers have mail programs built right into them. Here are links to tutorials on Microsoft and Netscape mail:

Microsoft Internet mail:
<http://hsc.csu.edu.au/help/software/email/tut/csu/>

Netscape 3.0 e-mail:
<http://uml.edu/tutor/using-nav3/direct.htm>

Microsoft Mail is now often replaced by
Microsoft Outlook.
Here is a tutorial for **Outlook Express:**
<http://wally.rit.edu/instruction/software/outexp/>

Netscape Mail is now often replaced by
Netscape Messenger.
Here is a tutorial for **Netscape Messenger:**
<http://wally.rit.edu/instruction/software/messenger>

Chapter 1

What Is E-mail?

Electronic mail (e-mail) is one of the most popular features of the Internet. It has long been a way of communicating with people all over the world. You can sit at your computer, type a message, send it out over the phone line, using a device called a modem, and have it delivered to a computer halfway around the world in a matter of seconds. Best of all, you do not have to use any stamps.

Most people will tell you that e-mail is free. Although it is true that you do not have to use any stamps and there is no direct charge for sending e-mail, there *is* a price tag that everyone pays, even if you never send an e-mail. The cost is built into the price of your Internet service subscription.

▶ Communicating Using E-mail

Anyone can send messages back and forth to friends and relatives. The recipients of the messages are usually happy to hear from you and will respond. However, if you are sending messages to professionals, politicians, entertainers, or other people who receive lots of mail, you may get ignored—unless you know how to communicate effectively.

Though I will cover features you can expect to find on almost any e-mail software package, I will not dwell on how to use them. If you know what mail can do, consulting your manual or a book to find out which button to click is a simple process.

Knowing how to address an e-mail message is certainly important, but knowing how to locate the people you want to send mail to—such as experts who can help you solve problems—is equally important. Knowing how to send a message, using Eudora, Netscape, Microsoft Exchange, or any of a dozen other e-mail packages is important, but it is equally important that you know how to ask for help in ways that make others want to help you.

Lost and Found:
Sometimes even an e-mail message will get lost somewhere. If that happens, you may have to send it again.

Just about everyone who has an Internet connection will learn how to use the e-mail software, but many people will never use it for anything more than communicating with friends, because they do not know how to communicate effectively. They may look for help, but not know where to find it. They may find that they send out messages for help or information but get nothing in return. In the next chapter we will take a look at how to communicate in ways that bring you results instead of an empty mailbox.

▶ Online Communication Beyond E-mail

When you think of Internet communication, you probably think of e-mail. E-mail is a great way to keep in touch with friends, but that is just a small fraction of the power of e-mail. How many different uses can you think of for e-mail?

- You can use it to contact experts and technical support people.

- You can subscribe to thousands of free e-mail discussion lists that deliver messages from people all over the world right to your mailbox.

- You can contact other people who have interests similar to yours.

- E-mail can be used to send pictures, programs, sound files, movies, and more. You can even use it to send messages to computers and have them send back information. You do not even need an Internet connection to have Internet e-mail.

- Though e-mail is the most-used form of person-to-person communication on the Internet, there are many other ways you can contact people and work online.

- There are online chat rooms where you can hold a conversation with someone on the other side of the world by typing messages back and forth.

- There are Web conferences where you leave messages for others. Some allow you to leave comments, and others allow you to carry on written conversations.

- You can use a microphone to talk live to people. If you have a video camera, you can even see them while you are talking.

- There are online paging services that let you know others want to talk to you.

- You can have face-to-face video conferences.

Whether you are interested in communicating with people for enjoyment or to help make your school career more successful, this book should give you a head start.

Chapter 2

Netiquette

If you had done something special and were going to meet the president of the United States to be congratulated for your accomplishment, someone would probably meet with you beforehand and carefully tell you about diplomatic procedures for the meeting. When you meet important people, there are things you should do and things you should never do. The proper way to behave in front of important people is spelled out in a set of rules known as diplomatic protocol.

If you were going to visit another country, you would be wise to find out the customs of that country. In some countries, things we do in the United States every day might be offensive to people living there. For example, if you tried hitchhiking in Iran, you might get run over. Holding out your thumb in the United States or giving the thumbs-up sign would not be offensive to anyone, but in Iran it is an obscene gesture.

Understanding other cultures is important. The Gerber baby food company had a hard time when it first started trying to sell baby food in Africa. Here in the United States, the cute baby on each container attracts buyers, but the company did not realize that in Africa it is

Manners Count:
If you plan to use the Internet, you need to learn how to be polite to other people online.

common practice to put a picture of the contents of the package on food labels. It gives a whole new meaning to the term *baby food*.

When Coca-Cola first came to China, it was given a similar sounding name, but the Chinese characters used for the name meant, "Bite the Wax Tadpole."

When you get on the Internet, you are not only communicating with people from different cultures all around the world, but also entering a world where there is an online culture with rules and procedures of its own. There are things you should do and things you should avoid doing. The unofficial rules of the Internet are known as netiquette. It does not matter whether you are writing e-mail, leaving

Internet Addresses | Communication Facts | How Can I Be Safe?

Netiquette has been around for many years. I do not think any one person has been credited with creating the rules, but many Web sites have been created on the topic.

NewbieNet Newbiehood and Netiquette
<http://www.newbie.net/Newbie_Pages/new34.html>

Here's a complete online book for netiquette.

<http://www.albion.com/netiquette/book/index.html>

Do you know what satire is? This Web site makes fun of all the things people do wrong, by giving all the *wrong* advice. Read carefully. These are things you should *not* do.

<http://psg.com/emily.html>

messages on a Web site, or typing live to someone on the other side of the world. There are rules of behavior that should be followed. Fortunately, most of them are common sense, but there are others that are not so obvious.

If you break the rules of netiquette, there are no Internet police who will pull you over to the side of the information superhighway and give you a ticket, but it pays to follow the rules.

Before we discuss the different ways you can contact others, let's take a closer look at some of the basic rules of netiquette, online behavior, and online safety.

▶ Ten Commandments for Internet Ethics

No, Moses did not use e-mail. These ten commandments come to us from the United States Computer Ethics Institute in Washington, D.C. <http://www.brook.edu/its/cei/cei_hp.htm>. It outlines proper behavior for computer use in many areas.

Your school may have an acceptable use policy (AUP) for computers. These AUPs are designed to take into account all kinds of computer use, not just the Internet. An AUP may be very long, complicated, and difficult to understand, but most computer use policies can be boiled down to ten rules.

These ten commandments are just a few examples of proper netiquette. Proper use of the computer, the network, and treating people with consideration and respect are very important.

Be Nice and Polite:
Take a moment to give your computer a hug. It couldn't hurt, and, okay, we like the attention. (Just watch out for our wires . . .)

Internet Addresses **Communication Facts** How Can I Be Safe?

1. Thou shalt not use a computer to harm other people.

2. Thou shalt not interfere with other people's computer work.

3. Thou shalt not snoop around in other people's files.

4. Thou shalt not use a computer to steal.

5. Thou shalt not use a computer to bear false witness. (Don't spread rumors or lies about people.)

6. Thou shalt not use or copy software for which you have not paid.

7. Thou shalt not use other people's computer resources without authorization.

8. Thou shalt not use or appropriate other people's intellectual property.

9. Thou shalt think about the consequences of the program you write. (Don't write virus programs or programs that are intended to do harm in any way.)

10. Thou shalt use a computer in ways that show consideration and respect.

▶ Flames

When people disagree with things that are said on the Internet, they sometimes say or write angry words. When they are face-to-face, they can usually work things out, but angry words in e-mail and especially in public forums can cause major problems. If someone says something nasty to you in front of a group of people, it is only natural to want to defend yourself, but if you do it in anger, the other person will probably respond the same way.

Put Out the Flames:
An angry e-mail message is usually called a flame. Be nice and don't flame anyone.

Angry e-mail messages are called flames. Flames can destroy a good discussion, and they never solve problems. If someone flames you in a public forum, don't flame back. Respond calmly and logically. Tell that person, if he or she is upset with you, to please write private e-mail to work things out. The other people reading both messages will view the flame as an immature way of handling disputes and will view your words as a mature way of handling things. You may not win the private argument with the person, but you will have won in the eyes of those reading the public messages. Don't try to handle anger with anger. That will settle nothing.

▶ Online Safety

Along with netiquette there are other rules of the information superhighway for young people. These rules are for your safety. If you don't follow them, you risk losing your privacy or worse. Remember

Internet Addresses | Communication Facts | How Can I Be Safe?

Your safety is important. Here are some Internet safety sites for you and your parents or teachers to visit:

<http://www.familyguidebook.com>

The FBI's Parents' Guide to Internet Safety
<http://www.fbi.gov/library/pguide/pguide.htm>

<http://www.safekids.com/>

that you are in touch with real people. Though most are honest people with good intentions, there are also troublemakers and criminals online.

I'm sure your parents have told you never to talk to strangers on the street. You must always be careful and alert when talking to strangers online. When communicating, follow these simple rules:

1. Never give personal information about yourself or your family to people online. If they are family or friends, they already know it. If they are strangers, they have no need to know it.

2. Never arrange to meet anyone privately that you have met online.

3. If you get messages that make you feel uncomfortable, show them to your parents or an adult that you can talk to.

Be Careful:
Not everyone on the Internet wants to be friendly. Do not give anyone your personal information.

Chapter 3

Adding Expression and Body Language to Your Mail

One thing you must always keep in mind when writing e-mail is that you are invisible to the reader. He or she cannot see your facial expressions, hand gestures, or body language. When you talk to someone in person, your facial expressions and gestures add meaning to your words. When you write, you are invisible. This can lead to problems and misunderstandings if you are not careful what you write and how you write it.

Sometimes you may write something as a joke that a person takes seriously. It is often difficult to express your emotions accurately with just the written word. Fortunately, there are many ways you can add meaning to your words in e-mail through the use of symbols.

▶ Emoticons

The most popular method of showing emotions is through the use of something called smilies or emoticons. The term *smiley* comes from the most popular symbol used in e-mail to express emotion. The term *emoticon* is a cross between the words, "emotion" and "icon."

By using three typed symbols you can create a

Internet Addresses | Communication Facts | How Can I Be Safe?

This is the unofficial smiley dictionary.

<http://www.eff.org/papers/eegtti/eeg_286.html>

In addition to smilies, this one covers other ways of expressing yourself.

<http://www.cmmei.com/smiley.htm>

The Unofficial Smiley FAQ

<http://www.newbie.net/JumpStations/SmileyFAQ/>

smiling face (sitting on its side) to indicate you have written something with a smile on your face. Here is the basic smiley: :-)

There are other standard expressions. Here are just a few you can use with your messages:

```
;-)       smile and a wink
;->       wink and big grin
:-(       frown
```

There are actually dozens of emoticons. Some get very artistic and complicated. However, there are only a few standards. If you know how to use Internet search engines you can type "smiley dictionary" as your search term, and you will find dozens of places to visit.

Showing Emotion:
By using emoticons when you type, you can let people know how you are feeling, and have a little fun at the same time.

▶ Shortcuts and Acronyms

Acronyms are letters that stand for words or expressions. They are often called Internet shortcuts. There are many commonly used acronyms for e-mail. Acronyms are particularly popular in chat rooms. Chat rooms are places where people can type messages to one another. We will learn about chat rooms later in this book, but whether it is e-mail or chat rooms, acronyms can help you say a great deal very quickly.

Here are some of the most common acronyms and their meanings:

```
fyi       for your information
btw       by the way
tia       thanks in advance
imho      in my humble opinion
lol       laughing out loud
```

Acronyms are used in all walks of life, and there are lots of acronym lists on the Internet. Here are a few that have nothing to do with e-mail but might be of interest to you:

Internet Addresses | Communication Facts | How Can I Be Safe?

The Air Force Reserve Lab's acronym dictionary is full of military terms.

<http://www.afrl.af.mil/dictionary.html>

Acronym Finder has more than 138,000 acronyms and their definitions, covering a wide range of topics.

<http://www.acronymfinder.com/>

Yourdictionary.com links to other acronym pages, as well an exhaustive list of Web-based dictionaries and other aids.

<http://www.yourdictionary.com/diction1.html>

▶ Other Ways of Expressing Yourself

Along with acronyms and smilies, there are other ways you can express yourself when you type. If you want to make a point you can SHOUT IT OUT. Typing in all capital letters is called shouting. It is very useful as a way of expressing yourself. However, shouting can also be very annoying.

SOMETIMES PEOPLE ARE JUST TOO LAZY TO USE PROPER PUNCTUATION AND CAPITALIZATION SO THEY TYPE IN ALL CAPITAL LETTERS ALL THE TIME THIS IS UNACCEPTABLE.

If you think reading the last few sentences was annoying, imagine trying to read an entire page like that. Typing in all lowercase letters, without proper punctuation, is also annoying, though not quite as bad as typing in all uppercase letters.

Remember that people on the Internet cannot see you, and if they do not know you, they may

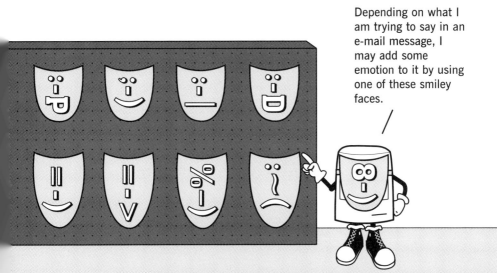

Depending on what I am trying to say in an e-mail message, I may add some emotion to it by using one of these smiley faces.

form an opinion of you based, at least in part, on the way you type your letters. Though casual e-mail does not require you to be perfect in your grammar and spelling, the more accurate you are the better the impression you will make. Many e-mail packages contain spell check features.

You may not have to worry about impressing friends, but if you want to get responses from letters you send to experts, professionals, and other people, you must be careful of what you write and how you write it.

There are many ways of expressing yourself. You can **emphasize** words with symbols. You can also show you have a smile on your face by placing a grin at the end of a line. <g>

You can make it a big grin <G> or a really big grin. <GRIN>

More Emotion:
When I finish writing a funny sentence, I like to end it with a big grin. <G>

Chapter 4

Getting People to Respond

Putting expression in your e-mail still does not ensure you will get a response. Actually, there is nothing that ensures a response, but there are things you can do to make your chances better. At some time in the future, you may have to contact someone you do not know for information.

For example, you may be doing a report on a topic and want to contact an expert for information. Many times, the expert you want to write to is the creator of a Web site you have visited. There is usually an e-mail address at the site. Other times, the expert will be someone you have located through places on the Internet that are designed to put you in contact with experts. A few such places are listed on page 22.

When you write, there is a right way and a wrong way of doing it. Here are some hints to help you get the response you want. Never contact someone for information until you have done everything you can do on your own to get the information. After all, would you expect a perfect stranger to take time out of his or her busy schedule to help you answer a question you could answer on your own?

Many of these people have jobs to do and are very busy. They cannot drop what they are doing to help someone without a good reason. If you want their help, you must give them a reason to want to write back. Here is a surefire way *not* to

Internet Addresses   Communication Facts   How Can I Be Safe?

The Virtual Reference Desk has links to dozens of experts on dozens of topics.

<http://www.vrd.org/locator/subject.html>

The teachers at the Marybutterworth School have created a page that links to dozens of experts on a wide range of topics.

<http://www.marybutterworth.net/expert.html>

Scientific American's Ask the Experts site has archived Q&A's for nine areas of science, current questions, and a form for submitting your own questions.

<http://www.sciam.com/askexpert/>

Do you have a question about volcanoes, earthquakes, mountains, rocks, maps, groundwater, lakes, or rivers? Ask-a-Geologist is the place for you.

<http://walrus.wr.usgs.gov/docs/ask-a-ge.html>

get a response from a cancer researcher. Just send an e-mail like the one on top of page 23.

Remember when I said people form an impression of you by what you write? Well, the person receiving this letter will probably feel you want them to do your report for you. Your entire message was less than a dozen words. You hardly spent any time writing it and did not show the expert that you even tried to help yourself. Do you expect the expert to write back volumes when you only took the time to write a single sentence? Besides, what should they write back? After all, cancer research is their job. Do you expect them to write everything they know in a single e-mail?

Asking for Help

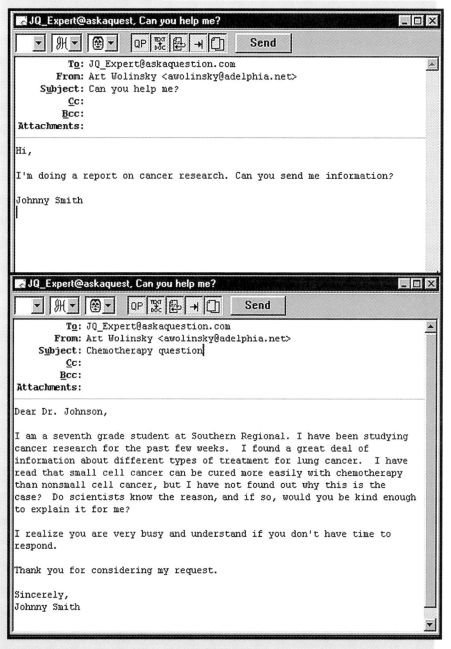

The top screen is an example of how not to get a response to an e-mail request. The bottom screen is an example of an appropriate request for information.

If you want someone to help you, you must help him or her to help you. You can do this by being specific about your questions. That way the expert can answer without having to guess what you need. You should also tell about yourself and your project.

The second letter on page 23 is more likely to get a response.

Getting Help:

If you ask a question politely, many times people will answer it as best as they can.

You do not have to be a genius to see which letter has a better chance of getting a response. It pays to be polite, and it pays to show the person you are writing to that you have been working hard to help yourself. Many people are willing to help students who are trying to learn and who make it easy to help.

Chapter 5

The Cost of Free E-mail

There is a popular belief that e-mail is free, but there is also a popular saying: There is no such thing as a free lunch. The computers, switches, cables, and people running the e-mail systems all cost money. Even though you are not paying for each message, each one has an expense attached to it, and everyone who uses the Internet shares that expense. Part of your monthly service charge goes to paying for the e-mail you send.

Junk mail I receive through the regular mail can be very annoying, but if the people who send it want to waste their time and money to send it, there is not a whole lot that can be done about it. On the other hand, junk mail in my electronic mailbox really annoys me, because the person who sent it did not even have to use a stamp. He or she sent me mail, I paid for it, you paid for it, and everyone else on the Internet paid for it. In many cases the mail is just a rip-off and a way for the mailer to get richer at the expense of everyone else on the Internet.

For example, I constantly get very well-written mail from people claiming that they got rich with this business or that business, and that I, too, can become rich. All I have to do is to send ten dollars for the details. Doesn't it make you wonder? If they are rich, why do they need my ten dollars?

When I was a young boy, I sent two dollars through the mail so I could get everything I needed to build a solar-powered clothes dryer. I could not wait to build it and surprise my mother. When the package arrived and I opened it, I was the one who was surprised. Inside was everything I needed, including instructions on how to hang the clothesline that came in the package. The solar-powered clothes dryer was a clothesline.

Remember, if it sounds too good to be true, it probably is.

▶ Spam

Probably the most expensive and most talked about e-mail abuse today is spam. I'm not talking about canned meat. Spam is electronic junk mail. Sometimes it is in the form of a get-rich-quick scheme or something that seems too good to be true. It can offer you thousands of dollars in income for a small investment of money and time. If you respond to spam, you are probably going to be disappointed and will lose whatever money you send. Remember, always be careful when you are online.

Too Much:
Unwanted e-mail messages can overflow your mailbox and make it difficult to find your important messages.

Spammers take advantage of people who are looking for an easy way to get rich. Someone may get rich, but it will not be you. Whoever sent that message probably sent hundreds of thousands just like it. It cost them next to nothing, and if they get a thousand people to respond out of hundreds of thousands of messages sent, they made a nice profit. They cheated people out of money, and everyone on the Internet shared the cost of sending all those messages.

The government is looking into ways to stop spam, and most Internet service providers will cancel the accounts of anyone they find sending spam.

▶ Hoaxes

Another serious problem on the Internet is e-mail hoaxes. These hoaxes are expensive practical jokes. The most common hoaxes revolve around e-mail viruses. Watch out for this type of hoax. If you get fooled, not only will you feel silly, but you will also be adding to the problem of overloaded mail servers. Here's how it works.

One day you may get a message that warns you not to open any e-mail with the subject line (description), "Good Times" or any one of a half dozen other subject lines. The message will go on to warn you that if you open the message, it will erase your entire hard drive. It continues by asking you to forward the message to everyone you know, but *don't do it!*

First of all, e-mail messages are text. Viruses are programs. Text can't harm your computer. There is no way opening a text e-mail message can erase your hard drive. Second, by forwarding the messages, you are clogging the Internet with junk mail. That *does* cause harm and additional expense. In addition, if you forward the message to a friend who knows this, you will probably get a reply telling you about how a practical joker took you in.

Real or Fake: Some e-mail messages are meant to trick you. You should look at each message closely to see whether it is a hoax.

Important Note

Though text messages cannot harm your computer, e-mail attachments can contain harmful programs. I mentioned earlier that e-mail could be used to send pictures, sounds, and computer programs. They are sent as attachments. The attachment must be opened separately from the e-mail. Attachments can contain harmful programs, but they cannot harm your computer until you activate them. Before you open an attachment, be sure you know who sent it and what it is. If you receive an attachment from an unknown source, I would advise you to delete it without opening it.

▶ Chain Letters

There are many chain letters circulating on the Internet. The get-rich-quick schemes I mentioned earlier are just one kind. There are others that may seem harmless, but they are not. For example, you may get a "Good Luck" message telling you to forward it to ten friends. If you do, you will have good luck. If you don't, you will have bad luck.

It's a good thing not everyone is superstitious, or the Internet would be in big trouble. Let's do a little math and see what could happen if everyone who received a chain letter responded to it within one hour. Let's say a chain letter starts by going to ten people. Those ten become one hundred an hour later. In two hours there are ten thousand messages; in three hours there are a hundred thousand messages. . . . At the end of eight hours there would be one billion messages. Even if the chain does not grow this rapidly, the result could be clogged systems and crashed servers.

Of course, not everyone responds to chain letters, and certainly not that quickly, but you can see that chain letters have the potential to be a serious problem, not just harmless messages.

▶ Urban Legends

Did you ever hear a story that was so great that you just had to repeat it? Urban legends are stories that sound as if they could be true, but they are actually too good to be true. They sound so great that people want to circulate them. They are written as true stories, and every once in a while one is really true, but most are just legends. As a result, they take on the nature of chain letters and clog up the mail. Here is one example of an urban legend.

Chain Letters:
Not everyone likes to receive a chain letter, even if it's through e-mail. Chain letters are usually not worth sending to someone.

Fire authorities in California found a corpse in a burned out section of forest while assessing the damage done by a forest fire. The deceased male was dressed in a full wet suit, complete with a dive tank, flippers, and face mask.

A postmortem examination revealed that the person died not from burns but from massive internal injuries. Dental records provided a positive identification. Investigators then set about determining how a fully clad diver ended up in the middle of a forest fire. It was revealed that, on the day of the fire, the person went for a diving trip off the coast—some twenty miles away from the forest.

The firefighters, seeking to control the fire as quickly as possible, called in a fleet of helicopters with very large buckets. The buckets were dropped into the ocean for rapid filling, then flown to the forest fire and emptied.

You guessed it. One minute our diver was making like Flipper in the Pacific, the next hc was doing a breaststroke in a fire bucket 984 feet (300m) in the air. Apparently, he extinguished exactly 5 feet 8 inches (1.78m) of the fire.

Some days it just does not pay to get out of bed!

It certainly sounds possible. Doesn't it? I do not have any idea of how many people this fooled, but it has found its way into my mailbox at least six times over the past few years.

▶ Other E-mail Problems

There is an old saying: Be careful what you wish for. You just might get it. You must always think about the possible consequences of your words when you

You can't believe everything you see or read on the Internet or in an e-mail message. Sometimes people will try to mislead you.

send out a request that will reach many people. Here are two cases where people were trying to do something good and it backfired because they did not fully understand the power of online communications.

Two students came up with what they and their teacher thought was a great project. They would ask people to send them a simple e-mail, with the objective of trying to collect e-mail from as many different states and countries as they could. What they forgot to do was set a closing date. Because the project seemed worth while, many people responded and responded and responded. The mail kept coming, and coming, and coming. There were so many pieces of mail that their school server crashed, creating many problems.

> **Think About It:**
> Don't believe every e-mail that you receive. Protect yourself against e-mail tricks, and you'll have a better Internet experience.

In another instance, the marketing department of a major book company came up with what they thought was a great way to help a charity and get free advertising. They started circulating an e-mail message stating that for every five messages received before Christmas they would donate a book to a children's hospital.

They set a closing date, but they never checked with the system administrator beforehand. Had they done so, he would have told them, their idea was not practical. The response was so great that the server could not handle the mail. It crashed and communications were down for quite a while. I assume it also cost the book company quite a bit of money for the donated books.

The solution to these problems is not simple. You might think that closing the e-mail accounts would do the trick, but that just makes the problem worse. Imagine you were receiving ten thousand letters a day through the United States mail. To get away from them, you might decide to move and not leave a forwarding address. That might solve *your* problem, but that means ten thousand letters a day would have to be returned to the senders. While you may have solved *your* problem, you *created* problems for many other people.

The only way the problems in the previous two examples were solved was through follow-up messages alerting people to the problem and asking them not to send any more e-mail. The incident with the school took place in 1995, and in 1997, occasional responses were still coming in.

Hoaxes and urban legends could be the subject of another book. They make very interesting reading. You can learn a great deal and also have a lot of fun reading about them. Here are some sites that can provide you with some interesting reading:

Internet Addresses | Communication Facts | How Can I Be Safe?

You can find out whether the threat is real or fake. Check the Computer Incident Advisory Capability, the Department of Energy division in charge of policing the Internet.

<http://ciac.llnl.gov/ciac/CIACHoaxes.html>

Along with virus hoaxes, you can find out about other urban legends at:

<http://urbanlegends.miningco.com/library/blbyolix.htm>

Some additional stories and guidelines can be found at:

<http://www.kumite.com/myths/>

What's in an E-mail Address?

An e-mail address has two parts separated by an @ sign. The first portion is the user ID as assigned by a system administrator when the account is established. In many cases, you can choose this part of the address yourself. As long as no one else on the same system is using it, you will be able to call it your own.

The part that comes after the @ represents the name of the computer that acts as your post office.

A question always arises about case sensitivity (matching uppercase and lowercase letters). E-mail addresses are usually not case sensitive, but many parts of the Internet do require exact matches. It is good practice to assume that everything is case sensitive. This will save a lot of frustration. As you become more comfortable with the Internet, you will learn which areas are case sensitive and which are not.

▶ Locating E-mail Addresses

Writing the most magnificent e-mail message of the century will do you little good unless you can send it to someone. Of course, you need an e-mail account and a way of sending the message, but you also need to know the recipient's e-mail address.

People often ask whether there is an e-mail

directory where they can look up someone's address. Well, there is good news and there is bad news. The good news is that, as with any other type of information on the Internet, there are search engines that can help you. The bad news is that there is no single place that has them all. So, finding a friend's e-mail address may not be that easy.

Internet Addresses   Communication Facts   How Can I Be Safe?

Here are three search engines that will help you find people:

<http://people.yahoo.com/>
<http://www.switchboard.com>
<http://www.whowhere.lycos.com>

Finally, here is a page that supplies you with some basic and advanced information and more links to finding people on the Internet:

<http://research.umbc.edu/~korenman/wmst/
    addresses.html>

Chapter 7

Mailing Lists

Did you ever have a pen pal or participate in a discussion group? Mailing lists are a combination of both pen pals and discussion groups, except with the help of a mailing list, you can have hundreds of pen pals and participate in dozens of discussions.

Internet mailing lists fulfill this function. You send *one* message, and *everyone* who subscribes to that mailing list gets a copy. Don't worry, subscriptions do not cost a penny, and no one will come knocking at your door, trying to sell you subscriptions to Internet mailing lists.

There are thousands of different mailing lists. Each mailing list has its own focus of interest. There are fun lists and there are academic lists. The bottom line is if you want to get in touch with people who have interests similar to yours, there is probably a list out there that fits your needs.

The biggest problem is often locating the proper list for you. That is not always easy. The list on page 36 provides some help to zero in on a list of your choosing.

▶ Subscribing

Finding a list is the beginning. Next you must subscribe to the list you have chosen. This means

Internet Addresses   Communication Facts   How Can I Be Safe?

The following Web site is user-friendly. Many lists have their own Web pages and offer forms that allow you to register online, rather than sending e-mail to a listserv (a dedicated computer).

<http://paml.alastra.com/>

The following site is probably the most comprehensive spot on the Web for locating mailing lists to fit your interests. It has information on more than seventy-one thousand lists:

<http://www.liszt.com>

This site is the official LISTSERV catalog, with the most up-to-date directory of lists. Lists can be searched by keyword or located by country or size of membership.

<http://www.lsoft.com/lists/listref.html>

Teachnet.com Mailing Lists and Listservs is designed for teachers, with activities, lesson plans, and list of mailing list and listservs for teachers. It also has a link to an even more comprehensive list of educational lists.

<http://www.teachnet.com/resources/mailing.html>

someone must process the subscriptions. That may be a person or a specially dedicated computer program known as a listserv. Regardless of whether you write your subscription request to a computer or to a human, there are certain procedures you must follow.

▶ Lists Administered by People

If you are writing to a person, there is usually no formal subscription format, but there are certain points of netiquette you should follow. If the e-mail address starts with listserv@, majordomo@, or listproc@, you know you are writing to a computer. Other than that you cannot be sure whom (or what) you are writing to until after you write. A person will answer you. A computer will send back a message indicating something went wrong.

When writing to a person, if there are no specific instructions provided, type SUBSCRIPTION REQUEST as the subject line and keep the message short, simple, and polite. The person on the other end is generally overworked and processing subscriptions in batches. He or she does not know you, and probably does not have time to indulge in idle chitchat that will interrupt that process. Save that for the appropriate time.

1. Simply make your request, such as:

Please subscribe me to the Porsche 914 mailing list.

2. Thank the person.

Thank you

3. Leave your name and e-mail address:

Web the Computer
MrWeb@anyaddress.com

▶ Lists Administered by Computers

Special computer programs called listserv, majordomo, or listproc administer many mailing lists. A listserv computer may handle thousands of lists without human help. It handles requests to subscribe, unsubscribe, and hold mail. It also acts as a copy machine and a post office. Listservs are really powerful, efficient, and fast. However, they cannot think. Everything must be perfect when you write a request to a computer. The computer has a very limited vocabulary. You must learn how to talk to the computer in its language, because it is incapable of understanding yours.

Once you find a mailing list that interests you, you subscribe to the list by sending a message to the listserv computer. When subscribing to a list administered by a listserv, you must do the following, substituting the proper information in place of the words: computer.name, list name, and your name.

```
To subscribe, send e-mail to:
        listserv@computer.name

In the body of the message put:
        subscribe List Name Your Name
```

For example, page 39 shows a picture of an e-mail message sent to subscribe to an imaginary mailing list I will call Science_Projects.

If you do everything right, the subscription will be processed and you will even receive a welcome message as one of your first messages. This message is very important. (*Do not throw it away. It contains information you will need later on.*)

If you do *anything* wrong, your subscription request will be rejected. However, all is not lost. If you make a mistake, the listserv will generate an automatic message with the rejection. It will cover commonly made errors and give instructions about the proper way to process your subscription.

A program called majordomo manages

Mailing Lists:
I like to look on the Internet for mailing lists that interest me, and if I find one I like, I subscribe to it.

Mailing List Subscription

| | Standard | ▼ | MIME ▼ | QP | | | →| | | **Send** |

To: LISTSERV@IND.CSE.EDU
From: Art Wolinsky <awolinsky@adelphia.net>
Subject: SUBSCRIBE
Cc:
Bcc:
Attached:

SUBSCRIBE SCIENCE_PROJECTS ART WOLINSKY

A subscription request to a mailing list on the Internet might look something like this.

some lists. If the list you want to subscribe to is a majordomo list, the procedure for subscribing is slightly different.

```
To subscribe, send e-mail to:
     majordomo@computer.name
In the body of the message put:
     subscribe List Name
```

▶ High Volume/Low Volume

Some lists deal with popular topics. As a result, they post many messages a day to your mailbox. When you subscribe to active lists, you often scan the subject lines, deleting large numbers of messages without even opening them. You may read only those messages catching your interest. This is an important reason for everyone to use good subject lines in e-mail messages.

High-volume lists can cause other problems, especially if you get them through your school e-mail account. If you get fifty to two hundred messages a day, keeping your mailbox unclogged can be a daily challenge, and then there are school vacations. If it is a ten-day or two-week break, you may have more than a thousand messages waiting for you when you return.

There is another very important reason for you to keep your welcome message in a safe place. It may have instructions on how to hold your mail. (Some lists do not have a hold function, and you may have to unsubscribe before vacation and then subscribe again when you return.)

▶ Points of Confusion

Get this straight. When dealing with mailing lists, there are always multiple e-mail addresses to consider. There is one address you use when you want to subscribe, unsubscribe, or hold your mail. There is another address if you want to send mail to everyone in the group. There may even be a list owner you can contact with specific questions. Of course, every message coming your way has been sent by an individual, and you may post your reply privately to the sender. A goof, embarrassment, or a disaster awaits the person who neglects to watch what he or she writes and to whom it is written.

For example, it would be appropriate for me to post a message such as this to the classic car list:

```
I'm looking for information on a
place in the New York, New Jersey,
or Pennsylvania area where I can get
my 1957 Chevy restored.
   Any information would be greatly
appreciated.

Art Wolinsky
awolinsk@concentric.net
```

Anyone who sees it and has information should reply to me at my private e-mail address (as included), *not* to the list.

Someone in Kalamazoo or Timbuktu has no interest in finding out about a restoration shop in New York, New Jersey, or Pennsylvania.

Be Careful:
Getting your name off of a mailing list can be tricky if you don't read the instructions carefully.

▶ Unsubscribing

Probably the most common annoyance is the person who sends a message to the list that should have gone to the listserv computer or to the list administrator. About once a week I can count on going to my mail and finding at least one message that simply says "Unsubscribe." When I see that, I know that someone did not save the welcome message, and I also know that the other twenty-five hundred list members got the same message.

Remember that your name is on every message. This is not the way you want to get your name known on the Internet.

Chapter 8

Two Alternatives to a Clogged Mailbox

Mailing lists have one major drawback. They can clog your mailbox quickly. Some high-volume lists can deliver up to two hundred or more messages a day to your mailbox. If you check your mail daily (or more often), you can keep up with the flow of mail, because you can use the subject lines to determine which messages you should read, and can often delete many of the messages without even reading them.

▶ Newsgroups

There are alternatives to mailing lists. One alternative is called a newsgroup. The purpose of a newsgroup is the same as that of a mailing list, namely, holding conversations with people who have similar interests. There is, however, a difference between the two. When you send a message to the listserv, the computer makes a copy of your message for each person on the list and then sends out one copy to each subscriber. If there are one thousand subscribers and fifty of them send messages, that means one thousand people each got fifty messages in their mailboxes.

When you send a message to the newsgroup, the message remains on the news server, and you read it by using a piece of software called a newsreader. In other words, instead of a listserv computer flooding your mailbox, you go to a news server and read the messages posted there. It's sort of like a giant bulletin board where you can read messages and then tack on your responses to any message, and anyone can tack on a response to your message.

There is another advantage to newsgroups. When mailing lists send you messages, the messages are all mixed together in your mailbox. If you subscribe to three or four mailing lists, the messages come into your mailbox and may be all mixed together. You may not know which messages are from which list until you open them. With newsgroups, each group is separate. You visit the groups one at a time to read and post messages.

Still another advantage is the fact that you do not have to subscribe to newsgroups and you do not have to search for them. Your Internet service provider will have a news server that will offer you thousands of newsgroups. All you have to do is logon to the server, find the newsgroup you want to read, and start reading.

All you need to read newsgroups is newsreader software. Most of today's Web browsers have newsreader software built right in, but many people prefer separate newsreader software. Separate software usually has more features than the reader built into browsers.

Newsgroups: Reading a newsgroup is like reading your favorite section of the newspaper—you get only the information you enjoy reading.

Finally, there is one way you can access the contents of newsgroups directly from the World Wide Web without having to access a news server or use newsreader software. Deja News <http://www.deja.com> is the only Web site

Both Microsoft Internet Explorer and Netscape have built-in newsreader functions. There are also many other newsreaders on the market. Here are a few examples:

Free Agent
<http://www.forteinc.com/agent/index.htm>

Win VN News Reader
<http://www.ksc.nasa.gov/software/winvn/winvn.html>

Newsreader.com
<http://www.newsreaders.com/>

where you can read, search, participate in, and subscribe to more than fifty thousand discussion forums and newsgroups.

▶ Web Conferences

Come Together:
With Web conferencing software, you can get together and chat with your friends.

As Web sites became more sophisticated, people figured out how to allow visitors to leave comments and participate in discussions. This knowledge led to the invention of Web conferencing software. This software allows the Web site owner to set up discussion areas where people can leave and respond to messages.

Each day, new Web conferences pop up. Each day, they gain in popularity, but it will be quite awhile before they challenge mailing lists or newsgroups. One of the main reasons they do not rival mailing lists or newsgroups is that, unlike mailing lists or newsgroups, there is no central place for the owners of the conferences to register them and no way to easily index them.

Some conferences are open to the public, and others are private. Many allow you to participate without providing information, but others require that you register.

Web conferences are great ways for groups of people to get together for projects or discussions that are temporary. For example, I set up a Web conference for people on a mailing list to experiment with. Here is a picture of what the conference looks like once you have entered your ID and password.

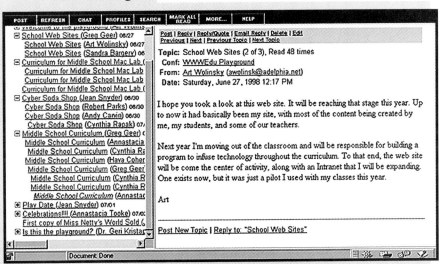

This is an example of a private Web conference area for a high school.

Chapter 9

Chats— Organized Chaos

Imagine what it would be like entering a room where there were twenty to thirty people standing around in small groups holding conversations. Now imagine what it would be like hearing all the conversations as they were taking place. Do you have that picture in your mind? Now imagine, instead of hearing the conversations, people were typing them and you could see everyone's words as soon as they finished their sentences.

You might see the start of three conversations, the middle of two others, and the end of others. Then you might see replies to any of the items that just appeared in front of your eyes. Do you have that picture in your mind? If it seems confusing, perhaps it will be clearer as you read on, but before I type another word, I want to make a few things very clear. Chat rooms can be a lot of fun, but you must be very careful when you enter any chat. You have no idea who the people you are talking to really are. The person who says he is a fourteen-year-old boy could very well be a fifty-year-old man, and the person who says she is a twenty-one-year-old college senior could be a sixth-grade student.

▶ Making Sense of the Confusion

What follows is a bit of conversation that took place in one of thousands of teen chat rooms. Examine it for a few moments, and then we will discuss what you see.

There are a few things that should be obvious. First, you will notice that there is not too much concern about capital letters or formal writing. Things happen very quickly in many chat rooms. If you take the time to type carefully, you will get lost or the person with whom you are talking will pick up a conversation with someone else.

Internet shortcuts are also used heavily. You will notice in these examples people will use "i" instead

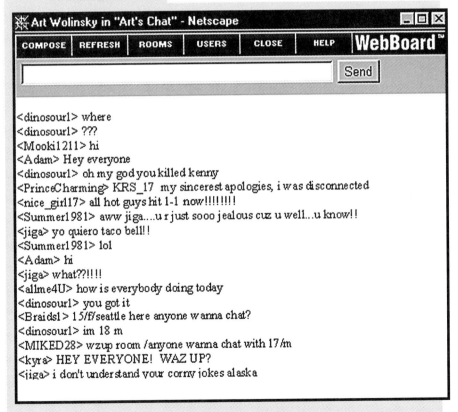

Chat Rooms

Art Wolinsky in "Art's Chat" - Netscape

| COMPOSE | REFRESH | ROOMS | USERS | CLOSE | HELP | WebBoard |

Send

```
<dinosourl> where
<dinosourl> ???
<Mooki1211> hi
<Adam> Hey everyone
<dinosourl> oh my god you killed kenny
<PrinceCharming> KRS_17 my sincerest apologies, i was disconnected
<nice_girl17> all hot guys hit 1-1 now!!!!!!!!
<Summer1981> aww jiga....u r just sooo jealous cuz u well...u know!!
<jiga> yo quiero taco bell!!
<Summer1981> lol
<Adam> hi
<jiga> what??!!!!
<allme4U> how is everybody doing today
<dinosourl> you got it
<Braidsl> 15/f/seattle here anyone wanna chat?
<dinosourl> im 18 m
<MIKED28> wzup room /anyone wanna chat with 17/m
<kyra> HEY EVERYONE! WAZ UP?
<jiga> i don't understand your corny jokes alaska
```

This is an example of a conversation that took place in one of thousands of teen chat rooms online.

You may have seen news stories about bad things that have happened to people who met someone on the Internet. Chat rooms are very often the place where these people first meet. Please be safe and follow these simple rules. (They are true for chats and all areas of Internet communication.)

- Do not participate in chats without first checking with your parents.

- Never give personal information about you or your family.

- Never arrange to meet anyone in person unless you are doing it with your parents along.

- If anyone says anything or sends you anything that makes you uncomfortable, let your parents or some other adult you trust know.

- Never get into arguments online.

of "I." They use "u r" in place of "you are," and they use "lol" quite a bit. "Lol" stands for laughing out loud.

Do things still look and sound confusing? Well, let's see whether I can clear up some of the confusion. Standing in a room with dozens of conversations going at the same time *is* confusing, but just as in the real world, you can focus on one conversation or participate in a one-on-one chat. Most chat rooms have a feature that allows you to page another person and have a private conversation with him or her. That will certainly cut down on the confusion.

Internet Addresses | Communication Facts | How Can I Be Safe?

Here is a short list of some of the common abbreviations used:

brb—be right back	ic—I see
bbl—be back later	cu—see you
afk—away from keyboard	cya—see ya
lol—laughing out loud	k—okay
rotfl—rolling on the floor laughing	lo—hello
j/k—just kidding	np—no problem
btw—by the way	tnx—thanks
ppl—people	plz—please

▶ Types of Chats

Only a few years ago, if you wanted to chat with someone, you had two basic choices. You could use something called Talk or Internet Relay Chat. The Talk function is built into Unix computer systems and allows one-on-one chats. There are many similar features built into other network software, but they see limited use. The most popular chat software, then and now, is Internet Relay Chat (IRC). However, IRC is getting more and more competition from Web chats and personal pagers.

Though there are different types of chats, they all rely on client-server software. That means you have a piece of client software running on your computer, and it makes contact with a server somewhere on the Internet. The server may host one chat room, dozens, hundreds, or thousands.

▶ Internet Relay Chat (IRC)

Internet Relay Chat started in the 1980s and is the most popular text-based client-server software. Since IRC is text-based technology, it may be a little more difficult to use than some of the newer software. It requires that you use typed commands to set up special features or to do many things. The commands look intimidating, but they are quickly learned. Newer software, such as Web chats and pagers, use pull-down menus and checkboxes for setup.

With IRC anyone can set up a server. (Well, anyone who can follow the instructions.) If you want to use IRC or other client-server chats, you will have to get the client software. These are usually free, and you can get them by visiting Web sites that provide software. The most popular clients are mIRC for Windows and ircle and MacIRC for Macs. However, there are many to choose from. You will have to decide which is the best for you. When you visit the sites, there are often reviews that can help you make up your mind.

Once you have installed the software, you can go to a directory of chat rooms or contact a friend. With

| Internet Addresses | Communication Facts | How Can I Be Safe? |

Here are some places where you can download IRC clients:

<http://www.tucows.com>

<http://winfiles.cnet.com/>

<http://shareware.cnet.com>

no additional fees and the ability to connect instantly, it is no wonder that chat rooms are so popular.

▶ Pagers or Buddy Lists

With most chat clients you must make arrangements to meet people online at a certain time, or you must look for your friends in chat rooms where they usually hang out. You can also go to directories and look them up. Buddy lists are new Internet tools that inform you who is online at any time, and they allow you to contact them whenever you want.

You do not have to go searching for your friends. The software does it for you. With these clients you can usually chat, send messages, files, and URLs, and play games. They are quickly becoming one of the most popular ways for people to communicate in real time.

▶ Web Chats

Instead of requiring a special client, your Web browser is the client for a Web chat. The browser works much like the other chat clients. The conversations scroll up or down the screen, depending on the chat server software.

Web chats are becoming more popular features on Web sites. Some Web sites feature hundreds of chat rooms. Others have just one. Some Web sites hold chat events. Chat events usually feature a well-known guest. That guest might be a movie star, a scientist, an author, a politician, or someone else many people would like meet.

After seeing the sample of what a chat screen looks like, you might wonder how any one person

Here are some sites where you can download buddy list software:

ICQ is the most popular buddy list software.
<http://web.icq.com>

After ICQ, the next most popular software is
AOL messenger.
<http://www.aol.com/aim/>

PowWow and Ichat are two other popular paging systems.
<http://www.activerse.com/>
<http://www.ichat.com/>

would be able to keep up with all of those lines flying across the screen. Actually, you might wonder *why* anyone would want to try to keep up with them.

The answer to those questions is simple. Nobody keeps up with all the conversations. First of all, if a famous person were online, you probably wouldn't be seeing the sort of chitchat you saw in the example. Second, events are always moderated. That is, there is a person in charge of the chat room, and there are rules for participation. In some Web chats, you type your questions and they do not appear on everyone's screen. They go to the moderator, and then he or she posts them when they are appropriate. In other Web chats, you let the moderator know that you have a question by typing a "?" as your message. They then add you to the queue (pronounced Q). A queue is a waiting area or waiting list. You will then be called on when your turn comes.

Chapter 10

Collaborative Software

There is software that allows you to have full-scale meetings online. You can not only chat, but also share a single document such as a drawing, and everyone in the conference can work on the same picture. The types of things you can do depends on the software you are using, but here are some of the features you might expect to find.

Chat: You already know about what you can do with chat.

Whiteboard: This is a drawing program. It functions very much like any simple paint or drawing program except that everyone in the conference can draw on it.

Guided Web Surfing: One person starts the Web browser session, and whatever page he or she goes to also shows up on everyone else's browser. So instead of telling everyone in the conference to go to a certain Web page, you can just go to that page and everyone else will automatically follow along.

Shared Applications: This is a relatively new but very important feature to watch for in the near future. It is similar to sharing the whiteboard except you share other programs, and all users can work on the same document at the same

Surfin' on the Net:
With the right software, you can surf on the Internet, and let other people watch.

Internet Addresses   Communication Facts   How Can I Be Safe?

Here are some links to conferencing software. You can visit the different sites and check out the features available with each software package.

Microsoft NetMeeting has a full line of features. This link also contains downloads of about twenty other conferencing packages.
<http://winfiles.cnet.com/apps/98/conf.html>

Netscape Conferencing is built into the latest versions of their Web browsers.

Habanero is a relatively new package developed by the National Center for Super Computing. It allows sharing of certain applications. You will have to read the instructions when installing this one. ;-)
<http://havefun.ncsa.uiuc.edu/habanero/>

The following site links to about one hundred more video conferencing software sites:
<http://www3.ncsu.edu/dox/video/products.html>

time. This does not mean *any* program can be shared. Right now only certain collaborative software has this feature, and the programs that work with the software are limited.

Voting: Some packages allow you to create a question, participants vote, and the software automatically totals and reports the results.

Voice Chat: This allows conference participants to speak with one another. Of course, your computer must be equipped with a microphone, sound card, and speakers.

Video Conferencing: This feature allows people in different parts of the country or world to talk to one another *and* see one another. You may think this is something you can never do because a television camera is not in your budget, but guess what? You can pick up some simple black-and-white television cameras for under fifty dollars.

Video Cameras:
If you buy a video camera, you might be able to let other people see you on the Internet. It's like being on TV!

Chapter 11

Where to Go and What to Do

Now that you understand how to communicate effectively and where to get the software tools you need, it would be a good idea to know where to go to contact people. In this final chapter I provide you with a wide range of places to go to communicate with other people.

▶ Pen Pals

There are hundreds of places you can go to find pen pals, but some are designed for adults, and some are really traps to get you to share information. Stick to major sites that are kid-friendly and safe. I have tried to provide you with only that type of site. There are four sites you can visit listed on page 57. There are also many other activities at these places in addition to pen pals.

▶ Kid-Safe and Family Chats

Similar to pen pals, many chat rooms are for adults, and many are places where troublemakers hang out. You should avoid any chat rooms that do not have clearly posted rules of conduct. The ones listed here are all designed to be places where you can have good, safe fun.

Internet Addresses   Communication Facts   How Can I Be Safe?

World Kids Clubs—Pen pals, chat rooms, activities, and games
<http://www.worldkids.net/clubs/>

KidsCom—Pen pals, chat rooms, writing activities, and contests
<http://www.kidscom.com/>

Kids Space Collection—A full-featured kids communication center
<http://www.ks-connection.org/>

Keypals Club International—Pen pals from all over the world are in this club started by twelve-year-old Lauren Dado.
<http://www.worldkids.net/clubs/kci/>

You can also locate a discussion group of interest to you through **Forum One**. It is an index of more than two hundred thousand Web-based forums.
<http://www.ForumOne.com/>

▶ Free E-mail

Often when you get an Internet account, you get one e-mail account with it. Rather than having to share a single account with the whole family, you can let your parents know about free e-mail accounts that you can access through Web pages. Everyone in the family can have their own private e-mail account.

Free E-mail Address Directory. The links that follow are just a few of the free e-mail servers. The next link has dozens of Web-based, free e-mail services.

<http://fepg.net/bytype.html>

Internet Addresses Communication Facts How Can I Be Safe?

Talk City has hundreds of chat rooms and many scheduled chats with authors, scientists, and celebrities.
<http://www.talkcity.com/>

i-Safe Connection has communications features for kids and teens.
<http://www.legalpadjr.com/msg/>

HeadBone Zone is a great kid site with loads of activities.
<http://www.headbone.com/friends/>

KidChatters features chat rooms and more.
<http://www.kidchatters.com/>

Curiocity's Freezone is a kid-friendly site for the curious.
<http://www.freezone.com/>

Cyberkids Connection is for kids under thirteen.
<http://www.cyberkids.com/cgi-bin/connection?15@@>

Cyberteens Connection is for kids thirteen or over.
<http://www.cyberteens.com/cgi-bin/connection?15@@>

Juno is the original free e-mail account, and you do not even need the Internet to get Internet mail. All you need is a Windows computer and a modem. It will ask for a lot of information. Be sure to get your parents' permission and have them help you with this.

<http://www.juno.com/index.html>

▶ Protecting Your Privacy and Your Wallet

Most of the chat rooms and many of the conferences are on commercial Web sites that make their money through advertising. The best ones designed for kids clearly mark all advertisements with an icon. Many others do not. Most advertisements come in the form of banners. Banners are rectangular pictures that often contain a cute phrase, contest, or something else designed to get you to click on it. When you click on a banner, you will be taken to that company's Web site. Once there, you may be asked for information.

Do not give out any information without your parents' permission. Winning a great prize might tempt you, but as always, you must be very careful when giving out any personal information on the Internet.

Here is a picture of a make-believe advertising banner. You will not see it anywhere on the Internet, but it gives you an idea of the size and shape of many banner ads.

Banner Ads

WEB ACTION FIGURES!

A limited time only! Click now!

At this time, this offer is not available on the following planets: Mars, Earth, Saturn, and Pluto.

This is an example of what an advertising banner on the Internet might look like.

Juniormail is another free e-mail service just for kids.
<http://www.juniormail.com/login/juniormail.asp>

Yahoo mail is becoming very popular.
<http://mail.yahoo.com/>

Hotmail is one of the early free e-mail accounts.
<http://www.hotmail.com/>

▶ Safety First and Safety Last

Remember, when you are using any of these communications tools, you are dealing with real people. You just cannot see them. Never say anything you would not say to someone's face. Do not be rude and do not get into angry conversations. Those types of behavior do no one any good and can get you into trouble. Keep a cool head and do not fight flames with flames.

See You Later . . .
Well, it's been fun, and we sure learned a lot about communicating on the Internet. I can't wait to do some more Internet surfing! See you soon!

Chats are fun, but chats can also cause problems. Be sure your parents are aware of your activities. If anything happens to make you uncomfortable, discuss it with them. If someone says something or does something that makes you uncomfortable, let your parents know.

Online communication and collaboration can be powerful tools for you in all phases of your life. Make the most of your online time and have good, safe fun.

Glossary

acceptable use policy (AUP)—Computer use policies that consist of basic rules of conduct.

acronym—A word formed by putting together the first letter of each word in a phrase.

banner—A rectangular picture that often contains a cute phrase, contest, or something else designed to get you to click on it.

case sensitivity—Matching uppercase and lowercase letters when typing.

electronic mail (e-mail)—The most-used form of person-to-person communication on the Internet. It provides a way to communicate with people all over the world.

e-mail hoaxes—Expensive practical jokes.

emoticon—A cross between the words *emotion* and *icon*, it is a popular method of showing emotions in an e-mail message.

flames—Angry e-mail messages.

guided Web surfing—A method by which one person starts a Web browser session and whatever page he or she goes to also shows up on everyone else's browser.

Internet Relay Chat (IRC)—A type of chat that was started in the 1980s. It is the most popular text-based client-server software and uses typed commands to do many things.

listserv—A specially dedicated computer program.

mailing lists—A combination of both pen pals and discussion groups except that you can have hundreds of pen pals and participate in dozens of discussions.

netiquette—The unofficial rules of the Internet.

newsgroup—A way of holding conversations with people on the Internet who have similar interests. It is comparable to a giant bulletin board where you can read messages and then tack on your response to any message.

protocol—Procedures or rules.

satire—Using humor or sarcasm to make a point.

shared applications—A relatively new feature that is similar to sharing a whiteboard except that you share other programs, and all users can work on the same document at the same time.

shouting—Typing in all uppercase letters in an e-mail message.

smiley—Another word for an emoticon.

spam—Electronic junk mail.

talk—A type of chat that allows one-on-one chats.

uniform resource locator (URL)—An Internet address.

urban legends—Stories that sound as if they could be true, but they are actually too good to be true.

video conferencing—Software that allows people in different parts of the country or world to talk to one another and see one another.

voice chat—Software that allows conference participants to speak with one another.

voting—A collaborative software package that allows you to create a question, have participants vote, and have the software automatically total and report the results.

Web conferencing software—A program that allows a Web site owner to set up discussion areas in which people can leave and respond to messages.

whiteboard—A collaborative drawing program that functions much like any simple painting or drawing program except that everyone in a conference can draw on it.

Further Reading

Computers and Children. Charleston, S.C.: Computer Training Clinic, 1994.

Henderson, Harry. *The Internet*. San Diego, Calif.: Lucent Books, 1998.

The Internet: How to Get Connected and Explore the World Wide Web, Exchange News and E-Mail, Download Software, and Communicate On-Line. DK Publishing, Inc., 1997.

McCormick, Anita Louise. *The Internet: Surfing the Issues*. Springfield, N.J.: Enslow Publishers, Inc., 1998.

Mitchell, Kim. *Kids on the Internet: A Beginners Guide*. Grand Rapids, Mich.: Instructional Fair, 1998.

Moran, Barbara, and Kathy Ivens. *Internet Directory for Kids & Parents*. Foster City, Calif.: IDG Books Worldwide, 1998.

Index